# THE PHANTOM
# IN THE MIRROR

# THE PHANTOM
# IN THE MIRROR

John R. Erickson

Illustrations by Gerald L. Holmes

Maverick Books
Published by Gulf Publishing Company
Houston, Texas

Maverick Books
Published by Gulf Publishing Company
P.O. Box 2608, Houston, Texas 77252-2608

10  9  8  7  6  5  4  3

Library of Congress Cataloging-in-Publication Data

Erickson, John R., 1943–
      The phantom in the mirror / John R. Erickson; illustrations by
   Gerald L. Holmes.
         p.   cm.— (Hank the Cowdog; 20)
      Summary: Hank the Cowdog investigates reports of a phantom
   dog on the ranch.
      ISBN 0-87719-231-6.—ISBN 0-87719-232-4 (pbk.).—
   ISBN 0-87719-233-2 (cassette)
      1. Dogs—Fiction. [1. Dogs—Fiction. 2. Mystery and detective
   stories. 3. Humorous stories. 4. Ranch life—Fiction. 5. West
   (U.S.)—Fiction.] I. Holmes, .Gerald L., ill. II. Title. III. Series: Erick-
   son, John R., 1943–   Hank the Cowdog; 20.
   PS3555.R428P45 1993
   [Fic]—dc20                                              92-35671
                                                                CIP
                                                                AC

This one's dedicated to
Lisa Rinker.
Welcome to the world.

# C O N T E N T S

C H A P T E R

# 1

# WHO'S FREDDIE?

It's me again, Hank the Cowdog. It was early December, as I recall, sometime between Thanksgiving and Christmas. It appeared to be a normal, ordinary day. At 7:05 I began my Barking Up The Sun procedure, and by 7:27 I had that job pretty well under . . .

Have we discussed the vicious rumors that have been circulating around the ranch lately? Maybe not. It seems that J.T. Cluck, the head rooster, has been whispering it around that HE is the one who causes the sun to rise.

The way he tells it, the sun wouldn't come up if it weren't for all the noise he makes in the morning—crowing, I suppose you'd call it—but there's absolutely no truth to his story.

Any sun that paid attention to a noisy rooster would be pretty silly, wouldn't it? No, it takes more

1

than a few squawks from a rooster to get the sun over the horizon. It takes the kind of deep and serious barking that comes from a Head of Ranch Security.

Anyway, it appeared that we had a normal day started . . . well, not really, come to think of it, because that was the morning I checked out a stray dog report.

Yes, that turned out to be a pretty exciting little episode but I don't think we have time for it here.

G.L.Holmes

I mean, we've got the whole Skunk Mystery before us, and then there's the part about the Phantom in the Mirror.

You ever run into the Phantom Dog? One of the scariest characters I ever encountered in my whole career.

Anyways, I was out there on Life's front lines, trying to bark up the sun, when all at once I noticed an echo. My barks were coming back to me, and that was odd. It had never happened before.

After a few minutes of this, it occurred to me that what I was hearing might not be an echo at all, but rather the sound of *another dog barking*.

Well, you know me. If there's a stray dog on my ranch, I want to know: A) who he is; B) exactly what he thinks he's doing on my outfit; C) who gave him permission to be there; and D) how soon he can leave.

Hence, once I had the sun pretty well barked up, I went swaggering out into the semidarkness to lay down the law to this trespasser.

"Hey, you! Who are you, and what do you think you're doing on my ranch? And by the way, I'm Head of Ranch Security, just in case you didn't know."

I stopped and listened. That's when I heard his reply: "Uh! Name Freddie and want make talk with ranch dog."

Hmmm. There was something familiar about the voice, yet when I ran "Freddie" through my data banks, I came up with nothing. According to my records, we had never had a "Freddie" on the ranch at any time.

I decided to probe the matter a little deeper. "Freddie, you're not in our files, which means you're not authorized to be on this outfit. If you're lost, maybe I can give you directions off the ranch, but for your own safety, I must warn you not to proceed any closer to the house."

"How come not closer to house?"

"Because, Freddie, this ranch is protected by one of the most sophisticated defense systems in the entire world. Get too close and the system kicks into Defend-the-House Mode, and once that happens, pal, I can't be responsible for your safety."

"Uh! Sound pretty stupid to me."

"Oh yeah? Hey, Freddie, take my advice and leave while you can still walk. The last mutt who trespassed on my place had to be scraped off two acres of sagebrush and carried away in a sardine can. I mean, that was all that was left of him. We're talking about serious consequences."

"Uh! Take 'cereal consequences' and stuff in left ear! Freddie not scared even a little bit."

I couldn't believe what I was hearing. Who was this guy, anyway? Whoever he was, he couldn't be very smart, and it appeared that I would have to contribute a little bit to his education, so to speak.

I mean, I don't go around looking for fights, but when stray dogs start mouthing off to me on MY ranch . . . hey, that's all it takes to start a riot.

"Listen, pal, it's clear to me you don't realize to who or whom you're speaking, so I'm going to give you one last chance. Get off the ranch and we'll drop all charges, write it off as a mistake, and forget that it ever happened. That's as good a deal as you're going to get out of me."

"Ha! Ranch dog full of baloney!"

HUH?

The hair on my back shot up. My ears shot up. My lips shot up, revealing deadly white fangs. A growl began to rumbling in my throat.

"Hey Freddie, did you just say what I thought you said?"

"Freddie say ranch dog full of baloney! And salami and prunes and brussels sprouts, ho ho!"

That did it. I might have overlooked the baloney but not the prunes and brussels sprouts. I lumbered out to teach this Freddie a lesson he wouldn't forget.

"Hey Freddie, I'm feeling generous this morning. Do you want to learn your lessons through normal pasture fighting or would you rather get an exhibition of dog-karate? I'm a black belt in both, by the way."

"Ha! Freddie feed ranch dog karate for breakfast!"

"Keep talking, guy. You're digging your own tombstone, and the more you talk, the deeper it gets."

You know what the mutt did then? He belched, real loud.

"Yeah? Well, some dogs learn easy, some dogs learn hard, and some dogs don't live long enough to learn much of anything."

"Yuck yuck! Momma of ranch dog big, fat, and ugly. Have wart on nose, wear gunnysack underpants."

I rolled my eyes on that one. This guy was really desperate for something to say. He must have been scared stiff.

Piecing together the bits of information at my disposal, I pulled up a profile of the little fraud. He had to be one of the pipsqueak breeds—poodle, terrier, Chihuahua. It's common knowledge that your pipsqueak breeds tend to be short of stature and long on mouth.

It's called The Little Dog Complex, if you want to get into the technical side. We've worked up personality profiles of all the different breeds, see, and we run into Little Dog Complex quite often.

In a classic case of LDC, you have a shriveled up, quivering, lickspittle runt of a dog who tries to do with his mouth what he can't do with the rest of his body. You can spot 'em right away and you don't even have to see 'em.

They all talk trash, and the trashier the talk, the smaller the dog.

This Freddie fit the LDC profile. I mean, he was a classic case right down the line. I was positive that, when I crossed the last little hill between us and looked down the other side, I would see . . .

HUH?

You know, one of the things that makes coyotes particularly dangerous characters—I mean, aside from the fact that they are cannibals and have been known to eat ranch dogs—one of the things that makes coyotes particularly dangerous enemies is that they can BARK just like a normal dog.

You wouldn't expect a cannibal to bark, would you? I mean, they're best known for their howling, right? That's what coyotes are supposed to do, howl.

But they're also famous for cheating, and one of their favorite cheating tricks is to bark like a dog. They do this to lure an unsuspecting ranch dog away from the house, don't you see, and it happens all the time, thousands of times each day in all parts of the country, and even the best and smartest of ranch dogs fall for it once in a while.

So it was no disgrace, no big deal that I . . . that our equipment came up with faulty profiles and so forth and . . . hey, they were CHEATING, don't forget that.

Okay. You'll never guess who I found waiting on the other side of that little hill. It wasn't a loud-mouthed little poodle, as you might have suspected, but Rip and Snort, the cannibal brothers.

They had lured me into an ambush, see, by cheating and lying and using cheap tricks, and by the time I figgered it out, they had already . . .

We needn't go into every detail. I, uh, gave them the whipping they deserved and hurried back to headquarters to, uh, finish up my morning chores.

I still had a lot of work to do.

There just wasn't time in my busy schedule for fighting and brawling and such childish things.

Hey, I'm a very busy dog and . . . never mind.

Let's just say that too many cannibals in the morning can ruin your day.

CHAPTER

# 1-A

## TRY IT AGAIN

Can we start all over?

It's me again, Hank the Cowdog. It was a normal day on the ranch, early December, as I recall. After barking the sun over the horizon, I went straight back to headquarters and saw no stray dogs or anything else out of the ordinary.

No fights, no scuffles, no violence of any kind. It was just a totally normal day, and at that point I was ready to launch my investigation into the Phantom Dog Mystery.

Maybe you're not familiar with Phantom Dogs, so let me pause here to . . .

All right, maybe I'm withholding a few shreds of information and taking a few liberties with the truth, but who wouldn't? Let's face it, getting suckered into a fight with two coyotes isn't something that most dogs can be proud of. It makes us look bad.

It's embarrassing.

Humiliating.

A humbling experience.

Who wants to be humble? Not me. Humble is what cats are supposed to be, whereas your better breeds of cowdog . . .

Okay, I'll tell you the straight story if you'll promise never ever to repeat it, and I mean NEVER EVER. If word of this ever got into the wrong hands . . . ears, I guess . . . if word of this ever got out amongst the crinimals of the underworld, it could have very serious consequences.

Have you sworn yourself to silence with a solemn oath? If not, you're not allowed to finish this story. Put your book away this very minute and go . . . I don't know what you should do . . . go sit in the corner and count to 50,000.

The main thing is, be quiet and don't peek or listen to the following Highly Classified Information.

All clear?

Those two coyotes thrashed me badly. I mean, we're talking about walking into a couple of buzz saws running at top speed. They not only thrashed me, but they made it look easy and had a great time doing it.

They may have used cheap tricks to lure me out there, but there was nothing cheap about the whipping they passed out. It was the best whipping money could buy.

Fellers, I got romped and stomped in so many different ways, I ran out of toes to count 'em. As I've said before, when it comes to tough, Rip and Snort are the champs of the world.

Somehow I managed to escape. How? Good question. Maybe they got bored, shooting baskets with me, but somehow I managed to escape their clutches and once that happened, we had Rocket Dog streaking back to the house—I mean, a cloud of dust and a puff of smoke.

I knew they wouldn't follow me up into the yard. They'd never been that brazen and bold before. They'd always chased me, oh, to the shelter belt and then turned back.

They chased me past the shelter belt, through the front gate, around the house, through Sally May's precious yard, out the back gate, and YIKES, they were still after me!

They'd never done that before. This was something entirely new, and where does a dog go when the cannibals chase him right to the house and through the yard, and where were Loper and his shotgun when I really needed them?

11

G.L. Holmes

My original plan had been to lose the coyotes up at the shelter belt, don't you see, and then return to my gunnysack bed under the gas tanks, there to wake up Drover and tell him of my morning adventures.

Instead, I went streaking past the gas tanks and yelled, "Hey Drover, would you come out here for a second, I need to tell you something!"

I felt it my duty to inform him that the ranch was under attack, don't you see, and . . . well, the thought did occur to me that his appearance on the scene might provide a, shall we say, diversionary tactic that might . . .

It didn't work. As I streaked past, he raised his head and muttered, "Murgle skiffer porkchop skittle ricky tattoo."

The coyotes didn't see him or weren't interested in eating him for breakfast, and the chase went on—back up the hill, through the front gate, through Sally May's precious yard, and things were looking pretty grim for the Head of Ranch Security, when all at once and thank goodness, Loper stepped out on the porch.

It appeared that he had come out to hang a Christmas wreath on the door, and in a matter of seconds I had taken refuge behind and between his legs.

That kind of surprised him. "Hank, what in the . ." And then he saw the cannibals. "Hyah, go on, get out of here!"

Well, they wanted none of Loper, even without his shotgun, and they pointed themselves east and set sail. At that point I ventured a step beyond Loper's legs and cut loose with a withering barrage of barking.

"That's right, and if you ever come into this yard again, I'll give you the other half of what I did to you out in the pasture! And you didn't fool me for a minute with that Freddie business."

I went all the way to the edge of the porch and barked until the cowards disappeared over that first hill east of the house, and then I barked some more, just to be sure they got the message.

(By the way, we've come to the end of the Secret and Classified Information. In a matter of seconds, the pages containing this highly sensitive information will hiss, sizzle, smoke, and disappear before your very eyes. Please stand back during this procedure).

HISS! SIZZLE!
SMOKE!
SELF-DESTRUCT PROCEDURE IS COMPLETED
PASSAGE HAS BEEN DELETED FROM MEMORY

Okay, where were we? Standing on the porch.

Loper whistled under his breath. "My gosh, that's the first time I ever saw coyotes come right up in the yard. They must be operating on short rations. Did you give 'em a pretty good whupping, Hankie boy?"

I . . . uh . . . yes. A good whupping had indeed occurred.

In other words, yes.

I'd given them the thrashing they so richly deserved, and even though it had appeared there for a moment that they'd gotten the upper hand, they'd actually gotten the, uh, lower hand.

They were lucky to have escaped with their lives, and next time, if they were foolish enough to try it again, next time they might not be so lucky.

I barked them one last time, just to give emphasis to my warning.

Loper grinned and scratched me on top of the head. "Pooch, it looks like you got a Mohawk haircut all the way from your ears to the end of your tail."

He was referring to the strip of raised hair on my back. In some quarters it has been said—incorrectly, as you'll see—it has been said that these so-called "raised hackles" reveal that a dog has just been scared beyond recognition.

Nothing could be further from the truth. Those reports are based on gossip, faulty research, and misquotations. Raised hackles and hair standing on end have nothing whatsoever to do with fear.

Rather, they are part of a dog's natural defense against, uh, severe cold.

Chill.

Loss of body heat.

Hypothermometer, it's called.

Don't forget, this incident occurred in December, and it can be very cold in the Texas Panhandle in December, especially in the early morning hours.

Extremely cold.

Bitter.

And loss of body heat can be a serious problem for a dog in this climate, why, if we didn't raise our hackles once in a while, the entire countryside would be littered with . . . well, frozen dogs.

It's that serious, so it should come as no big shock or surprise that I had my Thermal Hair Panels raised to collect the first warm rays of the sun.

It would have been foolish of me NOT to have initiated the THP procedure. In cold weather, we just can't run the risk of a total freezedown, and that's why . . . I think we've covered the Thermal Hair Panels.

Okay. There we were, Loper and I, together on the front porch, enjoying another glorious Panhandle sunrise. He was lavish in his praise of my handling of the Coyote Crisis and congratulated me for running the scoundrels off the ranch.

Then he informed me that I would have to handle all the ranch's business that day because he had been "drafted," to use his word, for . . . how did he put it? "Operation Honeydew," which meant that he would spend the entire day helping Sally May get the house, yard, and so forth ready for the church choir's Christmas party.

"Honey, do this. Honey, do that." Honeydew. Get it?

No problem there. I mean, running the entire ranch was no big deal for me, and I assured him through wags and barks that everything would be just fine.

I was about to leave when he said, "Hey, Killer, what's this?"

He seemed to be pointing a finger down at . . . hmmm, was that a small puddle of water? Yes, his finger seemed to be directed at a small puddle of water on the, uh, porch.

Our eyes met. "Is that some of your work? It ain't mine."

I, uh, gave my tail a slight wagging motion and . . .

Okay, remember those Thermal Hair Panels? You won't believe this but every so often, or actually more often than you'd think, they form tiny clouds of condensation, and under the right conditions, these tiny droplets of water will condense and fall to the earth—or to the porch—and actually form pools.

Or puddles.

Puddles consisting of natural mist and tiny droplets.

And so what we had there was just a simple case of water condensation caused by the raised . . .

It WASN'T what you think.

C H A P T E R

## 3

# THE PHANTOM DOG
# IN THE MIRROR

I left Loper to his "Operation Honeydew" business and got away from Sally May's yard as quickly as I could. I mean, this might have been the Christmas season and all, but a guy didn't want to take too many chances with her "peace and goodwill," not where the yard was concerned.

Now, it was okay for the cat to come and go as he pleased. He could lounge around the porch, sharpen his claws on the trees, rub on the legs of everyone who came out the door, and beg for scraps all day long. But let a dog set foot in the yard and suddenly the air was filled with sticks and rocks and harsh words.

It sure wasn't fair, and when I rounded the northwest corner of the yard and saw Pete up ahead, sitting in front of the machine shed, I decided to strike a blow for Fairness and Justice.

He was parked there on the gravel drive in front of the big double doors, see, had his tail wrapped around his hindquarters and was staring at a bird perched on the tin roof. Oh, and the last two inches of his tail were moving back and forth, a sure sign that he was up to no good.

No doubt he had it in his mind to capture and eat this bird, this poor innocent little sparrow. No doubt this poor innocent charming little song-bird had planned for months and months to fly south with all her little birdy friends, but perhaps she had learned at the last minute that one of her little wings was damaged and wouldn't carry her south with all the rest of her friends and rela-tives.

And her family. In a tearful ceremony, she had said goodbye to her five lovely children . . . her hus-band of many years . . . her devoted father who now cried teaspoons of tears . . . her poor old grandmother . . . the mother who had fed her worms and bugs and watched her grow into a beautiful charming lovely innocent little song-bird.

Oh, what a sad day that had been, as all the birds on the ranch had gathered for the long and dangerous journey to . . . wherever it is down south that birds go . . . South America, South Africa, South Texas, Abilene, somewhere down there . . . oh, what a sad day that had been!

And now Pete was staring at that same bird with his cunning yellow eyes, his heartless cunning yellow eyes, and flicking that last two inches of tail.

G. L. Holmes

This touching scene almost broke my heart, and since Rip and Snort had almost broke my face only minutes before, it seemed only fair and right that I should, heh heh, strike a blow for Fairness, Motherhood, and Wildlife, and give the cat the kind of pounding he deserved.

Because I never had much use for Pete in the first place. Have we discussed cats? I don't like 'em, never have, for reasons too numerous to mention.

So I went into Stealthy Crouch Mode and slipped up behind old Pete—he never saw it coming, never suspected a thing, tee hee—and I jumped right in the middle of him.

HISS! REEEEEEER!

Hee hee, ha ha, ho ho. He sprang into the air and turned wrongside-out . . . did manage to tag me in several spots with his claws, right on the end of my nose, in fact, which brought tears to my eyes, but they were tears of joy . . . I mean, a guy can't expect to get free entertainment in this life.

Yes, I did pay a small price, but hearing him hiss and yowl made every scratch worthwhile. And then I chased him up the nearest tree.

That was fun too. Wouldn't this be a sad old world if we couldn't chase cats up a tree every once in a while?

"Well, Pete, how's the bird business today?"

He looked down at me with his big cat eyes. "Mmmm, my goodness, I believe Hankie the Wonder Dog has just arrived."

"That's correct, kitty, here to protect our National Wildlife Heritage from the likes of you. You ought to be ashamed of yourself, picking on poor innocent sparrows."

He gave me a sour smile. "As a matter of fact, Hankie, they were picking on me. They've been dive-bombing me all morning."

"I'm, tee hee, sorry to hear that, Pete. Maybe you should quit staring at them, as though you were thinking of eating them."

"Me? Why, I wouldn't think of doing such a thing."

"Of course you would. You want a nice tender little bird for breakfast, but you're too fat and slow to catch one. Too bad, Pete, but don't get discouraged. Just remember: You might be slow but you sure aren't fast. Ho, ho, ho."

He rolled his eyes. "Somehow that doesn't make sense, Hankie."

"That's fine, because making sense with a cat isn't something I worry about. In fact, talking with a cat, any cat, is a waste of my valuable time."

He gave me that wierd cat smile of his—a smile that makes you think he knows a secret. "Oh, I'm not so sure about that, Hankie. Sometimes we cats see things that might be of interest to the Head of Ranch Security."

I couldn't help chuckling. "I doubt that, kitty."

"Mmmm, well, whatever you think, Hankie, but I can tell you that we cats are very observant." He turned his big cat eyes on me and grinned. "We see things."

My ears jumped to their upright position. I guess I had taken them off Manual Liftup and switched them over to Automatic, and in that mode they react to even the smallest of protuberations.

"What do you mean, you see things?"

"Oh, nothing. Nothing at all. I'm sure it would be a waste of your valuable time."

I noticed that he still wore that secret grin. He knew something, and I intended to find out what it was.

"Pete, if you've seen something suspicious, I'd advise you to report it at once. And quit grinning at me. That gives me the creeps."

"Have you been to the machine shed this morning, Hankie?"

"No, I haven't been inside the machine shed for two days."

"Hmmm, then you don't know about the Phantom in the Mirror, do you?"

"No, I don't, kitty, nor do I have any . . . what Phantom and what mirror?"

He took his sweet time getting around to business. Sitting up there in the fork of the tree, he licked his front paw, wrapped his tail around his haunches, and stared down at me.

"I'm waiting, cat. You're wasting my time."

"Patience, Hankie. What I'm going to tell you will be worth the wait."

"I'll be the judge of that."

"Because . . ." He widened his eyes and dropped his voice to a whisper, " . . . because I saw a very strange thing this morning."

"Never mind the dramatics, Pete, get to the point."

"I saw a dog in the machine shed."

"Impossible. If we'd had a stray dog on this ranch, I would have been the first to know about it."

"That's what I thought, Hankie, and that's what made it so strange. Maybe you were asleep."

"Lies, Pete, nothing but lies. And for your information, I wasn't asleep. I was out in front of the house, thrashing cannibals."

"Whatever you say, Hankie, but I saw a dog in the machine shed not thirty minutes ago."

My first instinct was to laugh at this wild story. In fact, I did laugh, but I noticed that Pete wasn't laughing. "You're serious about this, Pete. You're telling me an outrageous story that I can't possibly believe, but you're not laughing. That bothers me."

"Yes, it bothered me too. And I wondered what he meant when he said . . . oh, you wouldn't be interested."

I wasn't laughing any more. "You're exactly right, kitty, I'm not interested, but if he said something, I want to know what it was. Now."

"He said . . . let's see if I can remember how he put it . . . he said something about taking over the ranch."

"He said THAT?"

"Um hmmm, yes he did."

Suddenly I caught myself and realized that I had made a fundamental error. Just for a moment or two, I had allowed myself to get sucked into Pete's story. How could I have been so stupid?

ME, believe anything a cat said?

Yes, I had made an error in judgment but I had caught it just in the nickering of time. I marched a few steps away, took five deep breaths of air, looked at the clouds, and talked the hair on my back into laying down where it belonged.

Only then did I return to the cat and laugh in his face. "Nice try, Pete. I mean, that was a great story. No one can lie better than a cat. You've got a real talent there."

"Thank you, Hankie."

"But of course I don't believe a word of it. You didn't really think I would, did you? Why, that's the craziest . . . where did you see this so-called stray dog? I mean, just for laughs, I'd like to know."

He stared at me with those big unblinking eyes. "Near the north wall of the machine shed, there is a mirror with a wooden frame around it, like a window but not a window. I could see him in the glass."

"Oh, I see. You looked in a mirror and saw a dog. It gets better and better, Pete. I'm just sorry I can't stick around and hear the rest. Thanks for the entertainment and I hope you're enjoying the tree."

And with that, I wheeled around and left the cat sitting in the rubble of his shabby little scheme.

CHAPTER
4

# I IGNORE PETE'S STUPID STORY

I didn't give Pete's story another thought. The instant I walked away, it left my mind completely.

Instantly.

Totally.

Absolutely.

Without a trace or a memory.

Just as though I'd never heard it.

I mean, when you've been in this business as long as I have, you learn to disregard the testimony of cats.

Whereas your top-of-the-line, blue-ribbon cowdog will always tell the truth, never mind the consequences, your typical cat will go out of his way to tell a shabby distortion of the truth. I mean, they do it just for sport.

Which is why I have never paid the slightest attention to anything Pete . . . but on the other hand, it was kind of a fascinating lie. It showed some imagination and . . .

Phantom Dog, huh? Living in the mirror? I wondered where a dumb cat like Pete had . . . I mean, you wouldn't expect a dumb cat to . . .

But as far as giving Pete's story a second thought—no way. I had work piled up and investigations to make, and then there was the matter of supervising Mister Never Sweat, my assistant Head of Ranch Security, which would have been enough of a job in itself.

No, I had plenty of things to . . . take over the ranch, huh? You know, there are some things I'll tolerate in another dog, but when it comes to MY TERRITORY, I get real serious, real quick. I mean, the last dog who tried to take over my ranch . . .

Anyways, I didn't give it another thought. Within minutes I'd forgotten about it. It just went in one ear and out the other.

No problem.

I threw myself into a very busy schedule that would have exhausted three ordinary dogs. Hey, I was covered up with work! I barked at the mailman at 10:00, chased two cars and a pickup on the county road, rushed back to do a routine patrol of the corrals, and did some long-range observation of Loper as he struggled through Operation Honeydew.

He and Sally May stayed very busy down there at the house, raking the yard, picking up limbs, putting up Christmas lights, sweeping, and cleaning. This party for the church choir was looking more and more like a big deal.

At one point, around noon as I recall, I overheard Loper say to his wife, "Nobody's worth all this trouble. This is the last party we'll ever have."

But the important thing is that throughout the entire afternoon, I didn't give one minute's thought to Pete's yarn.

By five o'clock I was worn out and still had night patrol ahead of me. I trotted down to the gas tanks and found Drover curled up on my gunnysack bed.

Why can't Drover sleep on his own gunnysack? I don't know, but given a choice, he will always pick MINE.

"Arise and sing, Half-Stepper, and make way for the night patrol. And get out of my bed."

"Murgle muff mirk."

"Out, scram, be gone."

It took some pretty severe growling to get his attention, but at last he staggered out of my bed and fell into his own. At that point I fluffed up my gunnysack, circled it three times, and collapsed.

Oh, that felt good! I melted into its warm embrace, closed my eyes, and drifted off into . . . hmmmm. I couldn't sleep. Heck, I was tired enough to sleep, but for some reason . . .

I kept thinking about a stray dog in the machine shed. Yes, I knew that was ridiculous, but sometimes a guy gets a ridiculous thought in his head and he can't get rid of it.

So at last I gave up trying to sleep. I stood up, gave myself a good stretch, and decided . . . well, if I couldn't sleep, then maybe I ought to check out the machine shed.

For several days I had tried to work the machine shed into my busy schedule, and it had nothing to do with Pete's wild, improbable, silly story about the so-called Phantom Dog. I wasn't about to change my schedule, just to prove to myself that Pete was a chronic, habituating liar whose story I didn't believe.

In other words, Pete's story had nothing to do with my going into the machine shed that afternoon. I'd had it on my schedule for days. Weeks, actually.

A long, long time.

Checking out the machine shed was just a routine matter.

I did it all the time.

And so it was perfectly natural, perfectly normal that at 5:07 I poked my head into the space between the two sliding doors and peered into the half-darkness of the machine shed.

And I want the record to show that I didn't even look towards the mirror. No sir, didn't even think of looking at it. I had virtually forgotten Pete's stupid story anyway, and I had other things on my mind, such as:

A.

B.

C.

D.

Those were exactly the four items I had on my mind, and I'll come back later and add the details, because, well, they've slipped my mind at the moment.

But let the record show that I had four important things on my mind, not one of which involved checking out that mirror.

Okay. I poked my head through the crack in the doors, ran a quick Nosatory Scan, and sent the info to Data Control. The report came back and showed traces of diesel fuel, livestock mineral blocks, ordinary barn dust, and mouse leavings.

No major clues there, so I slipped through the doors and moved on silent paws across the cement floor. There, on that same cement floor, I came upon fresh evidence of cowboy activity: two welding leads, four stubs of welding rod, an empty pair of welding gloves, a welding hood, and several burn and splatter marks on the cement.

Someone had been welding. That was simple enough, but how did I know that the welder had been a cowboy? *Because he hadn't put his equipment back where he'd found it.* That was a dead giveaway. These cowboys around here are experts at getting out a bunch of tools and making a big mess, and then rushing off to something else.

That's a pretty poor way to run a ranch, if you ask me, but nobody ever does, so I'll keep my opinions to myself.

I picked my way through and around the debris, and continued my routine check of the machine shed. Everything appeared to be normal, and yet I couldn't shake the feeling that it was too normal and too quiet, almost as though . . .

At that moment I noticed a large mirror located near the north wall. I don't know what drew me over there to the gloomy shadow region of the shed, but suddenly I was grabbed by a feeling: *Somebody or something was lurking inside that mirror, and he was watching me!*

If you've been in security work as long as I have, you learn to pay attention to such unsplickable feelings. You don't have to understand them or know where they come from. You just listen to them, knowing in your deepest heart and mind that they have nothing to do with anything Pete the Barncat might have said.

So I zeroed in on the alleged mirror and began creeping towards it on ultrasilent paws: tail straight out, ears up in Max G (shorthand for "Maximum Gathering Mode"), and nose-radar working at top capacity.

Closer and closer I moved, hardly daring to breathe. The mysterious feeling that someone or something was present in the shed grew stronger with every step. Cold chills began rolling down my spine and the pulse in my ears was pounding like a drum.

Was I scared? Not really. I'll admit to feeling a certain sense of excitement. Tension. Aloneness. Foreboding. The awful silence of the place seemed to be closing in on me, and, all right, I might have been just a bit scared, but not much.

I had drawn to within six feet of the mysterious looking glass when suddenly I found myself staring into HIS eyes.

I, uh, didn't bark a challenge right away, but rather went to Full Reverse on all engines. After running backwards for a moment or two and stumbling over the stupid welding leads, I regained my composure and issued a stern bark.

At that point I faced a heavy decision. Should I return to the point of my deepest penetration into the machine shed and confront the Phantom Dog in the Looking Glass? Or should I leave the machine shed and go on about my business, confident that I had fulfilled the minimum requirements of a routine check?

Your ordinary run-of-the-ranch mutts would have shut 'er down right there, or maybe gone to the house to bark an alarm. Me? I wasn't quite ready to go public with this case until I had confronted the villain.

I mean, that guy in the mirror might have some crazy notions about taking over my ranch, and if that's what he had in mind, I figgered we might as well cross that bridge before we came to it.

And the sooner the quicker.

I went back for a showdown.

C H A P T E R

5

# OKAY, MAYBE PETE'S STORY WASN'T SO STUPID

As I approached the mirror, the Phantom Dog approached it too, but from the opposite direction. I stopped and barked and . . . maybe I retreated a few steps, but so did he. In other words, my barking had served notice on him that I wasn't a dog to be trifled with.

I studied his face and began the process of piecing together a profile. He had a big nose, much too long and crude to attract women in any large numbers. It might have made a good anvil, but it wasn't likely to take him far in the romance department.

The mouth told me a lot. It was drawn in the shape of a rainbow. At the ends of this rainbow were not two pots of gold but two hanging jowels. The mouth and the jowels combined to say that this dog took himself pretty seriously and didn't spend much of his time smiling.

There wasn't a lot of humor in that mouth.

His ears were no work of art, a little on the floppy side, seemed to me, but they were perked in such a way as to suggest that this guy was alert. In other words, I couldn't count on catching him off his guard.

Then I studied his eyes. They had a hard set about them that reinforced my observation of his mouth. His eyes contained a deadly combination of utter seriousness and arrogance. My guess was that this guy was vain, self-centered, self-preoccupied, and above all, a rather boring personality.

Oh, and one other thing the eyes revealed. For all his pretensions, this dog was not very smart. I felt much better on turning up this clue, knowing that I would be dealing from a position of superior intelligence.

At that point, after completing my profile, I decided that the time had come to open lines of communication with this arrogant fraud—and to order him off of my ranch.

I pulled myself up to my full height and massiveness and stepped up to the mirror, looked him squarely in the eyes, and beamed him a no-nonsense glare. I noticed that he tried to give me

G.L. Holmes

back the same kind of glare, but his wasn't very convincing.

"Hey, you. Give me your name."

He didn't answer, and at that point it occurred to me that he might not speak my language.

Have I mentioned that I'm flatulent in many languages? It's true, many languages. That's one of the things a dog must master before he becomes a Head of Ranch Security. And since I had this talent in my bag of tricks, I decided to address him in Ancient Egyptian, just to see if he would respond.

Here's what I said, in perfect Ancient Egyptian: *"Utt-whey izz-yeah oor-yeah aim-nay, ogg-day? Eek-spay!"*

(Translation: "Tell me your name and be quick about it, pooch, or you're liable to be picking up teeth all afternoon.")

He didn't answer—too scared, I would imagine—but I got the feeling that he understood this dialect, so I continued to use it. Here's what I told the imposter:

"Okay, the first thing you should know is that my name is Hank the Cowdog, Head of Ranch Security. This is my ranch and I've had you under surveillance from the moment you set foot on it. I've been watching you for days, and the only reason you're still here is that I've been busy with other matters.

"Point two: I've done a complete background check on you. I know, for example, that you call yourself The Phantom Dog, and you claim to live in this mirror. Don't bother to deny it, pal, I've read your dossier from start to finish."

He must have known that I had the goods on him. He didn't say a word, just stood there looking simple. And vain. By this time I had begun to feel more confident, and I bored into him with another piece of drill-bit evidence.

"Point three: Our background check tells us that dogs from your part of the world eat a lot of chickens. You might be interested in knowing that I saw your tracks in front of the chicken house this morning."

Now get this. I hadn't actually seen his tracks, but he didn't know that. I tossed it out to see how he would respond.

He responded just as I had predicted: his eyes wavered ever so slightly, and he ran his tongue over his chops. Both reactions are 100% accurate indicators of a dog who would like a nice chicken dinner.

I pressed on with my interrogation.

"So as you can see, Mister Phantom Dog, I have exposed your plot to raid the chicken house. The way I've got it figgered, taking over the chicken house was going to be the first step in your drive to take over the whole ranch. Am I right or wrong?"

He didn't answer. I mean, that dog was so shook up, he couldn't say a word.

"That's fine, you don't have to answer. I'll supply the answers and you can follow orders. I'm giving you two choices for your next move. You can either pack up and leave this ranch immediately, or you can stick around a while and risk the consequences. Which will it be?"

He just sat there, looking vain and arrogant and about half-stupid. Then, all of a sudden and you won't believe this, he STUCK HIS TONGUE OUT AT ME.

Hey, I might have considered working out some kind of peaceful solution that would have allowed him to leave with his dignity intacted, but that tongue-sticking-out deal kind of narrowed my options. I couldn't let him get by with that.

"Did you just stick your tongue out at me? You needn't bother to answer, pal, because I saw you, and you're now in deep trouble."

I pushed myself up on all fours and squared my enormous shoulders. And I'll be derned, he did the same thing.

"This could be your last chance to take it back. If you refuse, then I can't be responsible for what happens next."

He didn't take it back. Instead, he leered and sneered at me, which was further proof that he wasn't nearly as smart as he thought he was.

Okay, he'd been warned. I'd given him a chance to avoid a showdown. Now it was time to go to Sterner Measures. I paced back and forth in front of the mirror. So did he. I stopped and growled. So did he. I showed him teeth, and he did the same.

This was turning into a waiting game, a war of nerves. Apparently he lacked the guts to make the first move, while I, on the other hand, didn't want to make any rash decisions that I might regret later on.

There's a big difference between those two, believe me.

This must have gone on for several minutes, until I got tired of waiting. At that point I began a barking maneuver that was calculated to test his resolve. I began diving and lunging in front of him, while barking at the same time.

You've seen world champion cutting horses at work? Same deal, only cutting horses, even your very best ones, have never quite mastered the trick of barking at the opposition.

I barked and I snapped and I snarled. I lunged and weaved and dodged and parried, and when I was sure that I had confused him with this flurry of motion, I hit the Go Button and launched my . . .

B O N K !!

When I regained consciousness, I found myself lying in a heap on the machine-shed floor. Above me stood Drover, wearing his usual silly grin.

"Hi Hank, what are you doing down there on the floor?"

"I've just been mauled by the Phantom in the Mirror, you dope, and where were you when when I needed you?"

"Gosh, I don't know. What's the Famine of the Murr?"

"He's one of the biggest and most dangerous dogs I've ever encountered, Drover, and he tried to sneak onto the ranch through that mirror. I caught him in the act and gave him a terrible thrashing."

"I'll be derned. If you gave him a terrible thrashing, what did he give you?"

I glared up at the runt. "I had him whipped, Drover, but he landed a lucky punch."

"Must have been a pretty good lucky punch."

"I just hope that he hasn't taken over the ranch."

"Well, I just came from the gas tanks and I didn't see him down there. What does he look like?"

"Big, huge, arrogant, cocky. Covered with blood and scars and bruises, and I wouldn't be surprised if he was missing one of his ears."

"No, I didn't see him."

"I must have scared him off, Drover, which is the best news of the day. While you slept, this ranch had a narrow escape with disaster."

"Boy, I sure hate that I missed it. I wonder where he went."

I pushed myself up to a sitting position. My head and neck were very sore from the fight, and so was the tip-end of my nose.

"I don't know where he went. Peek into that mirror and tell me what you see."

"Peek into . . . you know, Hank, I'd be glad to do that, but this old leg of mine sure has been . . ."

"Peek into the mirror! That's an order."

"Oh rats."

He went creeping up to the mirror and very slowly poked his head around the side of it. At first he gasped and jumped back, but then he looked again.

"Oh my gosh!"

"What is it, Drover? Give me a complete description. Is it the Phantom of the Mirror?"

"Well, I saw a dog, but I don't think it's the one you saw."

"Oh? There must be two of them in there, perhaps even more. That could be bad for us, son. Give me a complete description."

He moved himself in front of the mirror, cocked his head to the side, and smiled.

"Drover, what are you grinning about? Tell me what you see, and hurry. We don't have much time."

"Oh my gosh, Hank, it's a handsome prince!"

C H A P T E R

# 6

# SOMETHING LURKING IN THE WEEDS

"A handsome prince? How do you know that?"

"Well, I can just tell by looking. He's handsome and brave and kind, and he looks like a prince. Hello there, Mister Handsome Prince. My name's Drover, and when I grow up, I want to look just like you."

In spite of my wounds and injuries, I pushed myself up on all-fours and hobbled over to the mirror. "Out of the way, Drover, I'll handle it from here. I happen to speak their language, whereas you can hardly speak your own."

"Well, he seemed to understand what I was saying."

"He was just being polite, Drover, and we can't risk blowing this historic opportunity. Now move aside before I have to go to more drastic measures."

"Well, okay."

I pushed him aside and stepped in front of the mirror. I was about to address this Handsome Prince fellow, when . . .

HUH?

"Drover, you moron, that's no handsome prince. That's the same guy who just beat me up!"

"I thought you . . ."

"Never mind what you thought. If he gets out of that mirror, we're in deep trouble."

"Oh my gosh, let's run to the machine shed!"

"We're already in the machine shed!"

"Oh, my leg!"

While Drover squeaked and limped around in circles, I decided that my best shot would be to speak to the Killer Phantom Dog and try to run a bluff on him.

"Okay, Phantom Dog, just stay where you are and don't try any funny stuff. This place is surrounded. I've got fifteen huge Doberman pinschers waiting in reserve, right outside the door. One word from me and they'll be in here, ready to attack."

He didn't say a word, just stared at me.

"I'm willing to withdraw my troops if you'll swear on your Word of Honor that you won't set foot on my ranch. That's the best offer I can make. What do you say to that?"

He looked pretty scared. I had a feeling that he was ready to make a deal, and it came as no big surprise when he nodded his head and began backing away.

It happened that I began backing away at just about the same time. He backed and I backed. "That's right, mister, just keep moving and we won't have any bloodshed. Come on, Drover, let's get out of here!"

I wheeled around and dived out into the sunshine.

We went streaking away from the machine shed and and took refuge behind the chicken house. In the process of making good our escape . . . retreat . . .

In the process of executing our Reverse Attack Procedure, we bulldozed several chickens who were foolish enough to stand in our way. They were pecking gravel and seeds and other garbage that chickens eat, and you should have seen them scatter when we went zooming across the gravel drive!

"BAWK, BAWK, BAWK!"

I loved it. Nothing in this line of work brings quite as much satisfaction as scattering chickens, unless it's treeing cats. That's fun too.

G. L. Holmes

On the west side of the chicken house, we collapsed and caught our breath. Only then did we dare to celebrate our victory over the Phantom Dog in the Mirror and his comrade, whom we knew only as "The Handsome Prince."

"That was a close call, Drover. One false move and those guys might have taken over this ranch. I figger they had a whole army in that mirror, just waiting to attack."

"No fooling? How did they get a whole army into a mirror?"

I couldn't help chuckling at his nativity. "Son, maybe you don't understand about mirrors. A mirror appears to be a flat surface, but it's actually a black hole that leads to another dimension of reality."

"I'll be derned. I knew something was funny, 'cause I felt more like I did then than I do right now."

"What?"

"I said, I feel more like I do right now than I did a while ago."

"Hmmm, yes. Obviously you fell under the influence of the mirror's powerful gravitational field, so it was natural that you noticed something odd."

"Yeah, that was quite a field of gravel. Kind of hurt my feet."

"Yes, it was a feat to remember. What's even more impressive is that we sent their entire army fleeing into the bottomless depths of the mirror."

"We sure taught 'em a lesson."

"Exactly. They won't forget us, Drover. We made them look pretty silly."

He rolled his eyes around. "Gosh, I hope they don't come back and try to even the score."

"Don't be ridiculous, Drover." In the silence, I found myself, uh, rolling my eyes around. "Yes, I hope we weren't too hard on them. Drover, do you ever get the feeling that you're being watched?"

"Sometimes."

"Do you have that feeling at this particular moment?"

"Well . . ."

"If you don't, just say no, that will be fine. In fact, I'd rather you said no."

"Well . . ."

I rose to my feet and backed myself against the side of the chicken house, just in case they tried to take me from behind.

"Something fishy's going on here, Drover. I don't want to alarm you, but I KNOW we're being watched by someone or some thing."

"I thought you didn't want to alarm me."

"I don't."

"Then quit talking like that!"

"I'm merely stating . . ."

All at once Drover's eyes bugged out. "Hank, oh my gosh, THERE'S SOMETHING IN THOSE WEEDS OVER THERE!"

I, uh, tried to run through the side of the chicken house, in hopes of building a new door, but the chicken house proved to be a little stouter than I had supposed.

I bounced off, hit the ground, leaped to my feet, and turned to face the attack of . . .

"Drover, unless I'm badly mistaken, someone or something is lurking in those weeds."

"Oh my gosh, I knew it, help, it's the Famine Dog and, oh my leg!"

"Quiet, Drover. Stop spinning in circles and listen to me."

He stopped spinning but continued to shiver.

"Chances are it's only a weed blowing in the wind, I'm almost sure it is. In fact, I'm so sure about it that I'm willing to let you check it out."

"Me!"

I placed my paw on his shoulder. "That's right, Drover. But always remember: I would never send you on a mission that I wouldn't take myself."

"Oh good, then why don't you take it?"

"Because you need the experience. Now go."

I gave him a shove with my nose and he went creeping towards the whatever-it-was in the weeds. He took ten steps, froze, spun around, and came trotting back.

"I did it, Hank, I checked it out and I wasn't even scared."

"See? I knew you could do it. Did you get a positive identification?"

"Oh yeah. It's only J.T. Cluck, and I'm so proud of myself!"

"Nice work, son, I'll take it from here." I went swaggering over to the weeds. "All right, J.T., you can come out now. We've recaptured this area and it's safe to return to your home."

J.T. poked his head out of the weeds and looked from side to side. "Where'd the rascal go?"

"He's gone back to where he came from, J.T., and I doubt that we'll ever see him around here again."

"You say you ran him off?"

"That's correct, and we did it without much effort."

"Huh. You must know something I don't know, 'cause that was the meanest darn guy I ever ran into. And he sure did stink."

"I'll need to ask you some questions, J.T."

"Sure, ask me anything. Ask Elsa, she saw the whole thing. I was just peckin' around for bugs, see, little black bugs, found a whole bunch of 'em up there by the water well, and Elsa, she seen this guy coming up behind me, and she said . . ."

"Can you give me a description?"

"Huh? Sure I can. They're little black bugs with six legs, and they're pretty tasty."

"I don't care about the bugs. Describe your assailant."

He stared at me and blinked his eyes. "Naw, I wasn't sailing. I was pecking for bugs, when all at once this guy . . ."

"Did you get a good look at him?"

"Get a look at him? Naw, my head was down. Who can see with his head down? Naw, I didn't get a look at the rascal, but I smelled him, and boy, did he stink!"

I studied the rooster with hard, cold eyes. "That's the second time you've mentioned the smell of the Phantom Dog of the Mirror. It makes me curious."

"That's good. Every ranch mutt ought to be curious about something."

"There's only one problem with your testimony, J.T."

"Oh yeah? What's the problem? I want to hear about it."

"You will, if you'll shut your beak."

"Elsa wouldn't approve of you talkin' to me like that, mister."

"Too bad for Elsa. The problem is that I met the same Phantom Dog myself, this very afternoon, and I didn't notice any smell whatsoever."

J.T. looked at me with those weird rooster eyes. "Oh yeah? Well, maybe that's because the guy I ran into was a SKUNK."

The word went through me like a bolt of cloth. Suddenly the investigation had taken on a new and sinister dimension which would lead to . . .

Well, you'll see.

CHAPTER
7

# J.T.'S SHOCKING
# REVELATION

J.T. Cluck, the head rooster, had just made a shocking revelation. It took me a moment to adjust to the news, then:

"What? A skunk in the machine shed? Why wasn't I informed of this?"

"You was probably sleeping your life away on that gunnysack, would be my guess, and besides that, no rooster worth his salt needs to go running to a fool ranch dog every time there's a little danger lurking on the place. I can take care of my own business, pooch."

"Maybe you can and maybe you can't, but the fact remains that you failed to report the unauthorized entry of a skunk on MY ranch."

"That's right, mister, and what do you aim to do about it?"

What I aimed to do about it was remove about five pounds of feathers from his tail section, which I did. I mean, who did that bird think he was talking to?

The Head of Ranch Security does not take trash off the cats or the chickens, period. It cost J.T. a bundle of feathers but he learned a valuable lesson about mouthing off to the wrong dog.

My goodness, you should have seen him jump and heard him squawk! It was very satisfying, just by George made my whole day better and brighter.

Of course, it brought my interrogation to a sudden stop, since J.T. went highballing back to the chicken house, but that was okay because I'd learned all I needed to know anyway.

Spitting feathers, I returned to the spot where my assistant was waiting. "Well, Drover, this tooey case has taken an interesting patooey twist."

"What?"

"I said, this feather has taken an interesting patooey."

"Oh."

"Twist."

"Twist what?"

"No, no. I said, this patooey has taken an interesting . . . I seem to have a mouthful of patooeys."

He stared at me. "Did you know that you've got a mouthful of feathers?"

"That's what I just said, Drover. Could it be that you weren't paying attoey?"

"I thought you said you had a mouthful of petunias."

"No, I did not say that. I said 'patooey,' not 'petunias.'"

"I'll be derned. What's a patooey?"

The runt was beginning to strain my patience. "Patooey is the sound one makes when one is spitting feathers."

"Oh. Well, that makes sense 'cause you've got feathers all over your mouth. Maybe that's why you were spitting feathers."

"I know that, you brick. Once again, you're repeating the obvious and beating a dead plow."

"Horse."

"What?"

"A dead horse."

"A dead horse? Where?"

"Well . . ."

"Hurry, Drover, we don't have a second to spare! Where's the horse?"

"Well . . . you said 'dead plow' and I think you meant 'dead horse.'"

"WHAT ARE YOU TALKING ABOUT?"

"I don't know, I'm all confused and quit yelling at me! I can't stand to be yelled at."

I took a deep breath, closed my eyes, and walked several paces away. "All right, patooey, let's start at the beginning."

"My name's not Patooey."

"I KNOW YOUR . . ." I caught myself and lowered my voice. "I know your name, Drover. What concerns me right now is whether or not you've gone insane. First you talked about petunias, then you said something about a horse that had been murdered in cold blood. Then there was some nonsense about . . . what was it?"

"A dead plow?"

"That's it. Drover, a plow can't possibly be dead because it was never alive to start with."

"I know but . . ."

"Let me finish. You see, Drover, death grows out of life, and life is what this life is all about. Is that clear?"

All at once his eyes seemed to cross. "I'm so confused, I think I'll go back to bed."

"No chance of that, son. During my interrogation of J.T. Cluck, I learned that we have a skatooey skunk running wild on the ranch."

"Oh my gosh! What's a skatooey skunk?"

I looked deeply into the huge vacuum of his eyes. "Are you trying to make a mockery of this investigation? Have you no respect for law and order? Is nothing sacred anymore? Tell me, Drover, because . . ."

My ears shot up. Operating entirely on their own, they had picked up the sound of the screen door slamming up at the house.

". . . because it could very well be scrap time up at the yard gate. In other words, drop everything and go to Red Alert. Unless we hurry, the cat might get some of our scraps!"

And with that, we went streaking down to the yard gate. We never did get around to finishing our conversation, but that was okay with me. Trying to carry on an intelligent, coherent, meaningful conversation with Drover can be very discouraging.

Sometimes I even think . . . oh well. There's no sense in beating a dead plow.

We went streaking up to the . . . I've already said that, but the important thing is that we got there before the cat did. I mean, we beat him BAD, which is one of the best things that can happen to a cat on our outfit.

Have we discussed cats? Maybe not. I don't like 'em, not even a little tiny bit, have no use for 'em whatsoever. A cat is a totally worthless creature, and if I were in charge of designing and directing the world . . .

You know, that's not such an outrageous thought, me being put in charge of the entire world. Just look at my record as Head of Ranch Security. It's pretty impressive.

I mean, any dog who can operate a ranch can operate something bigger. The world is bigger.

Therefore, it follows from simple logic that . . . well, maybe you get the drift.

So where were we? Oh yes, at the yard gate. Drover and I had gotten there first and were waiting for Sally May to come outside with our scraps.

Under Ranch Law, we were entitled to first dibs on the goodies, which on any given day might include roast beef trimmings (which I like very much), fatty ends of bacon (which I love), and several slices of burned toast (which I can live without).

Pete came slinking up to the gate—purring, holding his tail straight up in the air, and rubbing on everything in sight. He tried to rub on my leg.

"Get away, cat. That rubbing business drives me nuts."

He grinned up at me. "Hi, Hankie. Did you find the Phantom Dog in the machine shed?"

"I not only found him, kitty, but also gave him a thrashing and ordered him off my ranch."

"How interesting! Did he remind you of yourself?"

"Not at all. Not even a little bit. He was arrogant, overbearing, pompous, and not very smart."

Suddenly the cat choked. At first I thought he was having a seizure but then it appeared that he was only laughing.

G.L. Holmes

"I'm glad to see that you're enjoying this, kitty, but I'm afraid the joke is on you." The cat screeched with laughter and nodded his head. "Not only did you give an incorrect description of the Phantom Dog, but you neglected to mention that he was traveling with a companion—a small-ish white dog who called himself the Handsome Prince."

Drover stepped forward. "Yeah, and I saw him myself, didn't I, Hank?"

"That's correct, Drover, and you'll be rewarded for that."

"When?"

"Later." The cat went into another fit of laughter. I glared down at him, then turned my gaze on Drover. "This cat seems to have come unhinged, and I haven't even gotten to the part about the skunk."

"Yeah. I'll bet he won't laugh about that."

Pete stopped laughing, sat up, and wiped his eyes. "Oh my goodness, tell me about the skunk!"

"I was just about to do that, kitty. You see, after checking out your garbled report, we learned through our intelligence network that the Phantom Dog and the Handsome Prince released a fully-armed, heat-seeking, infrared, turbo-charged skunk on this ranch, and we have reason to suspect that he will strike at any moment."

The cat fell over on his back and howled with laughter. I shook my head. "Drover, did you find anything funny in what I just said?"

"It sounded pretty serious to me."

"I agree. So what's wrong with this cat?"

"I don't know. Maybe he's just dumb."

"Well, yes, of course. We knew that all along, but there's more to it than that. I'm beginning to wonder if he's come down with some terrible disease such as Turkeylabosis."

"Gosh, what's that?"

"The victim begins to act like a crazed turkey, Drover. It strikes without warning and there's no cure for it. The disease just has to run its course."

Still laughing, the cat struggled to his feet and staggered down the hill towards the gas tanks. We watched and shared a moment of sadness.

"Poor old Pete!" said Drover.

"Yes, even a cat deserves better than this. But we must go on with Life's journey, Drover."

And with that, we tore our attention away from Pete and turned to the sad business of eating his share of the scraps.

C H A P T E R

# 8

# FISHING TURNS OUT TO BE NO FUN FOR ME

It wasn't Sally May with a plate of scraps. It was Little Alfred, her son. He had come out of the house and had started playing in the yard.

He had taken down the piece of plywood that covered the crawl space under the house, don't you see, and appeared to be playing Explore The Cavern. I had played that game with him on several occasions. It was a good game, but we had gotten into trouble over it.

Why? Because Alfred's dad didn't want the crawl space open and exposed. It attracted skunks, see, and a skunk under the house is no fun.

A skunk under the house is real bad.

Well, right away I saw two things I didn't like about the situation. The first was that Alfred had opened up the crawl space, and the second was that he didn't have any scraps.

I should have known. This was the wrong time of day for Scrap Time.

Scraps, you see, are composed of what's left after a meal at the house. At the present moment, we were in that time interval between lunch and supper. Hence, no scraps. Hence, the slamming of the screen door had been a false alarm.

That was disappointing. I mean, when a guy gets his taste buds all tuned up for some roast beef trimmings and fatty ends of bacon, it's hard to go back to Life's dull and monotonous rhythms.

Life without scraps is bearable, but also pretty boring.

"Well, Drover, it appears that we answered a false alarm."

"Oh drat. I sure was looking forward to some scraps."

"Yes, this could very well be a scrapless night for us, but at least we beat the cat to the false alarm. On a scrapless night, when Life loses all meaning, I guess that means something."

"It means I'm starving."

"It means you complain too much, Drover. Be happy with what you have and don't worry about what you don't have. That's a simple formula for a good and happy life."

"But how can life be happy without scraps?"

I aimed a steely gaze at the runt. "Will you dry up? You're starting to make ME unhappy. Until you started whining and complaining, I was a happy dog. I was content with my life. I was counting my blessings."

"How many did you have?"

"Hundreds. Thousands. I had thousands of blessings, Drover, but you've ruined them all, simply by pointing out that no dog can be happy without scraps. And now I'm just as miserable as you are and I hope that makes you happy."

"Well, that's not what I had in mind."

"Good. Great. You're getting just what you deserve, and we'll just sit here and be miserable together."

Boy, were we miserable! We were probably two of the unhappiest, miserablest dogs in the whole entire world, facing the long, cold winter night without a single scrap. Or even the hope of a single scrap.

Fellers, things were looking pretty bleak.

At that moment, Little Alfred saw us and came over to the yard gate. He had gotten tired of "Explore the Cavern," it appeared, and was looking for another form of amusement.

He looked at us through the wire gate. "What's the matter, Hankie? You wook sad."

Sad? Hey, sad didn't even come close to what I was feeling. On the other hand—I wagged the last three inches of my tail—on the other hand, there was nothing wrong with me that a nice juicy steak bone wouldn't have fixed.

Or a strip of steak fat, say three-four inches long. Or some roast beef trimmings. Or, shucks, even a piece of baloney. I mean, we weren't talking about truckloads of food, just a little token reward to get me through the long winter night.

Anyways, I wagged my tail and hoped that the boy might get the message: "Hankie needs scraps. Hankie will look very happy when scraps arrive."

I guess he didn't get the message, because he said, "Well, you want to go fishing wiff me?"

Fishing?

I ran my gaze across the back yard, searching for a body of water that might be large enough to support a fishing expedition. Just as I had suspected, there was no body of water.

In other words, no, I didn't want to go fishing—first, because fishing in a yard without water was impossible, and second, because I was too busy being miserable and unhappy.

Nix on the fishing.

"Well," said the boy, "I think I'll pway fishing."

Oh, so that was it. He was going to *play* fishing. Nope, I still wasn't interested. I had gone fishing with Slim on several occasions and it had been pretty boring, to tell you the truth.

I mean, you sit on the bank and watch a cork for hours and hours. Is that fun? Ha. No thanks.

And besides, I didn't dare enter Sally May's Precious Yard. You know how she is about dogs in her precious yard. She would never understand the business about fishing. Never.

"Well, I'm going to find me a piece of stwing and some bait, and then I'm going to catch me a big old fish."

He dashed into the house.

Fine. He could catch all the "big old fish" he wanted, and he could do it without my help because I had exactly zero interest in fishing.

I turned to Drover. "Well, are you still unhappy?"

"Yeah. Life's pretty awful sometimes. How about you?"

"Same here. It all seems so pointless, without scraps."

Little Alfred came bursting out the back door. In one hand he held a piece of string, maybe five feet long. In the other, he held a piece of . . . something. Bait, I supposed, but I really didn't pay attention because I really didn't care.

Fish bait might be interesting to a fish but it holds no fascination for a dog.

The boy sat down in front of the gate and began tying the alleged bait to one end of the . . .

Suddenly my ears shot up. My nose shot up. My eyebrows shot up. Unless I was badly mistaken, my nose, which is a very sensitive instrument, had just picked up the smell of . . .

I leaned forward and studied the bait in Alfred's hand.

BACON? A strip of raw bacon?

Have we ever discussed fishing? I love to fish, always have, even when there's no pond and no fish. I mean, who cares if you catch a fish? That's not important. What's most important and meaningful about fishing is that it gives you a chance to *be with the kids.*

Watch 'em grow up. Meeting a challenge. Having some good, clean, wholesome fun.

Fishing is a great thing to do with the kids, and maybe I haven't mentioned this before, but sharing the, uh, precious moments with these kids is a very important part of my job as . . . that was bacon, all right . . . important part of my job as Head of . . .

These kids grow up SO FAST! Before you know it, they're grown up and gone, and you look back and wonder why you never took the time to . . .

The smell of that fresh bacon was about to drive me bazooka!

. . . why you never took the time to share those precious simple moments, and by George, I needed to take that boy fishing!

I whined and whapped my tail, moved my front paws up and down, and even took the drastic action of jumping up on the yard gate—something I rarely do, for obvious reasons.

Sally May doesn't approve.

But I did it anyway, because . . . hey, she'd understand. She'd be proud of me for wanting to go fishing with her Little Alfred, the only son she had in the whole world, and guarding him against . . . well, you never know what kinds of hazards and dangers an innocent child might encounter on a fishing trip.

Alligators. Crocodiles. Huge snakes. Child-eating catfish. Lockless Monsters.

Fishing is very, very dangerous for children, and he needed me in there to supervise, and finally he got the message and opened the gate and let me in.

I, uh, went straight to the hand that held the . . . well, the bait, I guess you might say.

He pushed me away, "No, Hankie, get away. You can't eat my bait."

Eat his . . . I guess he'd gotten the wrong idea. He thought I wanted to eat his bait! Ha, ha, ha. Can you imagine that? Oh boy, these kids get the craziest . . .

No, nothing could have been farther from the . . . why, the thought never entered my . . .

See, the thing is, the boy had this so-called "bait" clutched in his hand, and any careful parent or guardian will tell you that . . . hey I needed to check it out, that's all. It might have been some dangerous substance.

Poison. Toxic waste. Flammable material.

I had to know.

Suddenly, the back door flew open and out came Sally May.

"Alfred, where is my electric mixer? Have you been playing with my mixer again? Because if you have, I'm going to . . ."

Let me pause here to say that there is something about Sally May that strikes fear in the hearts of dogs and little boys. Even if we haven't done anything naughty, her appearance on the scene makes us all squirm with guilt. And when we find ourselves in her yard, where dogs are not allowed, it makes us squirm even more.

When Drover caught sight of her, he dropped his head and started slinking away. Alfred dropped the string, clasped his hands behind his back, and began whistling. Me? Well, I ...

Snap. Gulp.

I ran a quick test on the Possibly Toxic Bait, shall we say, and holy smokes, that was some WONDERFUL bacon and it brought new meaning and purpose into my life!

Sally May placed her hands on her hips and glared down at us. I hoped she would be proud of me for taking such good care of her boy, her only son in the whole world.

And just to be sure that she understood the importance of my mission, I gave her my most innocent smile.

Huh?

I'll be derned. It appeared that I had a piece of string running right through the middle of my smile.

# 9

# ONE THING LEADS TO ANOTHER

She didn't look quite ready for the party, seemed to me. I mean, she was dressed in a housecoat and slippers, and she had her hair wrapped up in a turban made of a pink towel.

Perhaps she had just stepped out of the shower and was in the process of getting herself ready for the evening's festivities. Yes, that would explain why she had put makeup on only half of her face, while the other half remained . . . I don't know, pale maybe?

Yes, pale, and it was a strange combination—a little scary, to tell you the truth. For a moment there, I considered barking at her, but only for a moment. Barking at Sally May didn't strike me as a very smart thing to do, especially when she was running late and trying to get ready for a party.

So, even though she looked a little wild, I didn't bark at her.

She glared at her son. "Alfred Leroy, WHERE IS MY ELECTRIC MIXER? Have you been playing helicopters with it again? I've told you and told you and told you: Play with your toys and leave my kitchen equipment alone!

"You see what happens? Here I am trying to get ready for a Christmas party and the whole choir will be arriving at my doorstep in . . ." She glanced at her watch. "Oh my stars, they're going to be knocking on my door and I'm going to be running around the house in my slip, trying to find . . . WHERE IS MY ELECTRIC MIXER?"

The boy looked up at the clouds. "Well, wet's see."

"I have a dessert that needs whipped cream and I can't whip the cream without my mixer. Now, what have you done with it? Think, Alfred, this is very important."

The back door opened and Loper stuck his head outside. "Hon, a car just pulled up in front of the house."

Sally May's head flew back and her eyes grew as wide as fried eggs. "WHAT? They can't be here already. I still have thirty minutes!"

"It's Charles Mack and Sara  You know them, always early."

"Oh, how can they do this to me!"

"And I can't find any dress pants."

"I laid them out on the chair!"

"Hon, I know you did, but Molly spread peanut butter all over the front."

"Peanut butter! How could she . . . I thought you were in charge of Molly."

"Well . . . somehow she got into the peanut butter while I was reading *The Cattleman*. Anyway, I probably ought to wear pants to this deal and . . . oops, got to go. Someone's at the door."

Sally May's eyes were getting wilder by the moment. She turned back to her son. "Alfred Leroy, if you don't tell me where you put my electric mixer, I'm going to . . ."

Her words hung in the air like a hammer that was about to fall, but it didn't. Instead, her gaze seemed to move from Alfred to . . . well, to me, you might say.

"Is that dog *eating string?* Hank, how can you be so dumb?" Back to Alfred. "Where is my mixer? I want it NOW."

"Well, wet's see. I was pwaying wiff it."

"I knew it, I knew it, Alfred, I've told you . . . where is it!"

"I think it went . . . to the car."

She stared at him in disbelief. "The car? You put my electric mixer in the car? Why!"

"Well, I was pwaying hiwwycoptoos wiff it, and it just fwoo into the car, Mom."

"I can't believe you'd do this to your own mother, on the very day she's . . ." Her eyes stabbed me again. "And you! You're eating string. Why do we waste money on dog food? Get out of the way, dog."

I whapped my tail on the ground and tried to . . . but she was late and in a hurry, and she breezed past me and opened the back door of her car. She grabbed the mixer and started back to the . . .

I refuse to take responsibility for being in the way. I was just sitting there, minding my own business and wondering what five feet of string was going to do to my internal plumbing, and . . .

First thing, she stepped on my tail. I yelped and tried to move out of the way, never suspecting that in the process of trying to get out of the way of her thundering slippers, I would get in her way even more. But that's what happened.

And of course she got her legs tangled up and went sprawling into the grass, while Little Alfred snickered behind his hand. (She should have spanked that boy.)

Well, let me tell you something. When the lady of the house takes a dive into the grass, a true Head of Ranch Security doesn't just sit there looking simple. Our usual procedure in these situations calls for the dog to bark several times, and then to

G.L.Holmes

rush to her side and give her a big juicy lick on the face.

I leaped to my feet, issued several loud barks, and rushed to the scene of the accident. I was about to administer the proper Red Cross-approved CPR lick on the face when . . . her face had turned bright red, don't you see, and her upper lip had curled just enough so that I could see exposed fangs, and . . .

I, uh, cancelled the CPR lick on the face. I had a feeling that it wasn't right for this situation, so I licked Little Alfred in the left ear and let it go at that.

"Hank, can't I take a step in this life without stumbling over you?"

Me? What . . .

"And Alfred, it's NOT FUNNY! You go into the house right now and stand in the corner for five minutes."

Little Alfred headed for the house, while Sally May picked herself up off the grass.

Well, she was definitely stirred up about being late for her own party and it was definitely bad luck that I happened to be sitting there at that very moment.

I don't know who or whom she might have blamed if I hadn't been there, but I was, so naturally, out of all the dogs in the world, she chose to heap the blame upon me.

I smiled up at her, hoping that she might . . . why was she looking at me that way?

"Come here, you nincompoop. I won't have you running around the ranch with that ridiculous string hanging out of your mouth. What if the guests saw you, what would they think?"

I, uh, couldn't answer that.

"They'd probably think the truth—that we're raising the dumbest dog in Ochiltree County. Come here!"

Boy, that hurt. I mean, Sally May had made cruel and cutting remarks about me before, and I knew that our relationship had gone through its share of ups and downs, but for her to suggest that I was the dumbest dog in Ochiltree County . . .

It really hurt, cut me right to the crick.

I lowered my head, tucked my tail between my legs, and went to her. Our eyes met. I wagged my tail and gave her my most innocent wounded look.

"Stop eating string. We spend our hard-earned money, buying you dog food, and you don't need to eat string, for crying out loud."

She got a firm grip on the string and pulled. She probably shouldn't have done that.

Of course she had no way of knowing that I had . . . uh, just run an important test on a hunk of bacon, or that it was tied to the other end of the string, or that pulling on the string would set off a chain reaction in my digestive system.

In other words, she can't be blamed entirely for what happened next.

But neither can I. I mean, there I was, minding my own business, trying to digest my bacon and string, bothering nobody, asking no favors from . . .

Everything would have turned out fine if she hadn't pulled so hard on the string, if she'd given it a steady, slow pull. That would have brought the alleged bacon to the surface, so to speak, without disrupting my bodily processes.

But she was mad and late and in a rush, and she gave it a big yank.

And what was I supposed to do? Sit there and be a perfect dog while she was jerking around on my innermost innards and vital parts? Hey, my body is a very sensitive piece of machinery and you can't yank and jerk on it like it was a bulldozer or something.

As I say, she shouldn't have done that, but she did and you can probably guess what happened. I did my best to hold back the tide of . . .

Suddenly I was seized by this powerful convulsion, this sweeping irresistible tide of . . .

Once things start going sour, they just seem to stay that way. I mean, her shoe and foot could have been anywhere else on the ranch and . . . what lousy luck that she would have her shoe and foot right there in my path, at the very moment when . . .

Boy, was she MAD! Who'd have thought that she would actually chase me around the yard in her bathrobe, at the very moment when her guests were arriving for the Christmas party? I wouldn't have thought it, but she sure did.

I managed to escape but by the thinnest of margins.

And all of that over one measly piece of string.

Remind me never to go fishing again.

C H A P T E R

# 10

# AN IMPORTANT MISSION FOR DROVER

I took refuge in the feed barn and remained in deep dark hiding until I was absolutely sure that Sally May had given up the chase.

Only then did I dare to stick my nose out the crack at the bottom of the door—the same one, you might recall, that was warped at the bottom. I cocked one ear, gave the air a thorough sniffing, and ventured outside.

Darkness was falling and my stomach began to growl, reminding me that I hadn't eaten a bite all day. Well, I'd eaten one bite of Tricky Bacon, but that had done me more harm than good.

To my surprise, I saw Drover sitting nearby, staring up at the clouds. He gave me his usual silly grin.

"Oh hi, Hank. Was that your stomach growling?"

"Yes, as a matter of fact, it was. I'm starving."

"Yeah, me too. I would have gone to the machine shed and eaten some dog food but I was worried about the Famine Dog."

"Phantom Dog, Drover, and yes, I too wish we could go to the machine shed, but I share your concern about . . ."

Suddenly I heard an odd sound. I cocked my ear and listened. "Wait. Did you hear that?"

"Hear what?"

There it was again. "It sounded like a rusted gate hinge. Did you hear it?"

"Oh, that. It's just my old stomach growling. It must be thinking about a nice big bowl of Co-op dog food up at the machine shed."

Just then, my stomach growled again. "Yes, I see what you mean. It's getting kind of noisy around here, isn't it?"

"Yeah, it sure is. I hope we don't starve to death. What are you doing down here?"

"Hiding from a crazed ranch wife who just tried to commit murder on me."

"I'll be derned. Why would she do a thing like that?"

"Good question, Drover. As near as I can tell, it all began with a small misunderstanding, and from there, one thing led to another."

"Yeah, things do that sometimes. First you have one thing and that leads to two. Then you have two things and . . ."

"By the way, Drover, where were you when Sally May started blaming me for everything she hadn't blamed on me before?"

"Well . . ."

"You vanished, that's where you were. You left me there, all alone, to be blamed for crimes I didn't commit. How could you do such a thing?"

"Well, it was pretty easy. I just picked up and left."

"Yes, left your friend and comrade all alone on the field of battle. Drover, you ought to be ashamed of yourself."

"Yeah, I was a rat to leave. I feel pretty bad about about it already."

"And those things only get worse."

"Yeah, I'm not sure I can stand the guilt."

I placed a paw on his shoulder and spoke to him as father to son. "But I think I can help you out of your terrible trap of guilt and remorse and shame."

"Oh good! It's about to get me down."

I patted his shoulder. "We need a volunteer to go into the machine shed to check for phantoms." His eyes crossed. "And you're just the guy we've been looking for."

"Yeah, but . . ."

"Congratulations, Drover. You've been selected for a very important mission."

"Yeah, but . . ."

"I will be very proud of you, and all your guilt feelings will melt away like snowflakes. Everything has worked out for the best."

"Yeah, but . . ."

"Come on, trooper. A bowl of delicious dog food awaits us if your mission is successful."

"Yeah, but what if it's not?"

"If it's not, Drover, then you have my solemn word of honor that you will receive all the postnasal decorations the Security Division has to offer."

"Oh my gosh!"

We headed for the machine shed in a long trot. Well, let's put it this way: I was in a long trot but Drover soon fell behind. It seems that he had developed a serious limp.

"Boy, this old leg is really giving me fits! I'm not sure . . ."

"That's fine, Drover. All you have to do is limp over to the mirror and check it out. Once we get the All's Clear, All's Well signal, then we'll gorge ourselves on delicious dog food. A little limp here and there won't hurt a thing. Actually, it might even be better."

"Better than what?"

I slowed and waited for him to catch up. "Better than spending the rest of your life as a coward and a chicken liver. Believe me, Drover, this is an opportunity of a lifetime. It's your chance to prove what you're really made of."

"I already know what I'm made of. That's what scares me."

"Rubbish. All you have to do is scout the machine shed."

"Yeah, but what if the Famine Dog's still there?"

"Uh, well, we could find ourselves in a combat situation."

"Who's WE?"

"We, Drover, the entire amassed forces of the Security Division, standing together in a united front. Or to put it another way . . . YOU."

"Oh my leg!"

"I'll be standing by in a support position. Someone has to run the command post and attend to the complex details of coordinating the attack and maintaining communications and so forth."

"Maybe I could . . ."

"We all have our jobs, Drover, and unfortunately some of us have to take the ones without the glamour of combat."

"That's the one for me."

By this time we had reached the machine shed. I waited for Mister Limp to catch up. "Hurry up, son, it's getting dark. We don't have time to waste. Get in there and check it out."

He whined and cried but I stood firm and pushed him through the crack between the big sliding doors. He went creeping inside and I began the Mark and Count Procedure. I would give him three minutes to complete his mission. If he didn't return by that time . . .

Well, we could always give him another three minutes. There's no sense in rushing into things. Haste makes waste.

I had just marked two minutes and thirty seconds when his nose appeared at the door. "Yes, yes? What did you find? Give me a complete report."

He sat down on the gravel drive and looked up at the sky. "You know what I think? I think what we saw in the mirror was . . . ourselves."

I glared at the runt. "That's the most ridiculous thing I ever heard, absolutely the most . . . why do you say that?"

"Well, because it was my face in the mirror. I just know it was."

"That's absurd, Drover, because what you've chosen to ignore is that a mirror is actually . . ."

Hmmmm. I began pacing. Was it possible . . .

The pieces of the puzzle began falling into place. Who had given me the original report about the Phantom Dog? PETE. Who had laughed himself silly when we'd told him about the Phantom Dog and the Handsome Prince? PETE.

G.L. Holmes

Why, the sneaking little weasel! The no good, backstabbing, counterfeit little . . .

"Okay, it's all coming clear now, Drover. It appears that we've been tricked by the cat. He set this whole thing up to get back at me for running him up a tree this morning."

"I'll be derned."

"He'll pay for this, but in the meantime, Drover, we must take an Oath of Secrecy. The outside world must never know what we've done. Hence, if the subject of the Phantom Dog ever comes up again, our story will be that we were misquoted."

And with that, I closed the Case of the Phantom Dog and turned all my attention to the overturned hubcap just inside the machine shed door. It contained . . .

It was supposed to be filled with Co-op dog food, but it appeared that someone or something had been stealing our rations.

"Drover, have you been eating dog food?"

"Oh heck no, I was scared of the Food Phantom. Maybe it was Pete."

"I don't think so. The little sneak would love to steal from us, but I happen to know that he has trouble chewing our food. No, it wasn't Pete, I'm pretty sure of that."

"Well, maybe it was the skunk."

"Skunk? Oh, you're probably referring to J.T. Cluck's wild, improbable story? No, and let me explain why. In the first place, the skunk report came from a chicken, and that speaks for itself. In the second place . . . do you smell something?"

He sniffed the air. "Not really, but by siduses have bid actig ub on be ladely."

"Hmm. Maybe it was nothing. As I was saying, that skunk report was hogwash. We now know that the skunk couldn't have come out of the mirror and . . . are you SURE you don't smell something?"

He took a deep breath and cocked an ear. "You know, I think there's an odd smell around here."

"I was thinking the same thing myself, Drover. Would you care to guess what it might be?"

"Well, I'd hate to guess and be wrong."

"This is strictly off the record. Go ahead and make a stab at it."

"I'd guess . . ."

You'll never guess what he guessed.

CHAPTER

# 11

# THE DOG FOOD THIEF

Drover guessed that the strange odor had come from a skunk. What did you guess? Not a skunk, I'll bet.

My eyes began probing the gathering gloom of the machine shed. "You know, Drover, I had a feeling all along that we might find a skunk in here. It fits the pattern: first, the missing dog food, and now, the powerful smell."

"Oh my gosh, do you reckon he came out of the mirror?"

"We don't know the answer to that, Drover, but he's here amongst us, and he must be driven out of the machine shed at once. Otherwise, we might lose our precious food supply and spend the rest of the winter eating grass and tree bark."

"Yeah, and I hate vegetables. But how are we going to get him out of here?"

I had to think on that one. "Very carefully, Drover. It's a well known fact that skunks are easier to find than to herd. They don't herd well at all."

"I heard that."

"It takes just the right touch. Too little force and they won't leave. Too much force and . . . POW! The machine shed could be toxic and contaminated for weeks."

"Yeah, and us too."

"Exactly. The skunk must go, but we want him to feel happy about leaving. I'd better handle this one myself, Drover."

"Oh drat."

"You can back me up. Don't make any sudden movements or loud noises. Pretend that you're carrying delicate crystal gambits or rotten tomatoes."

"Okay, but what's a gambit?"

I glared at the runt. "A gambit is a special kind of glass. The slightest jar could cause it to shatter."

"Yeah, and jars are made of glass too."

"Exactly, so we must be very careful."

"I thought a gambit was a kind of robber."

"No. You're thinking of bandits."

"No, bandits are what you put on cuts and scratches."

"You're thinking of Band-Aids, Drover, and that's all the time we have for questions. We've got a job to do."

"Yeah, hauling rotten gambits and busted jars."

"Hush, Drover. You take a good idea and run it into the ground."

Some dogs dread Skunk Patrol. Me? I kind of enjoy mixing it up with a skunk every once in awhile. It's a challenge, a type of sporting event like a game of Rushing Roulette.

On the one hand, they're not very impressive fighters, so a dog doesn't run much risk of getting his ears torn off. Fighting is always more fun under those conditions.

On the other hand, a skunk doesn't have to be a great fighter because he's got something else up his sleeve—that bag of poison gas for which he is famous. And therein lies the challenge: seeing how far you can push one without getting sprayed.

Yes, once in awhile a guy presses too hard and gets his smell changed, but that's just part of the risk and part of the fun. And it's not so bad, once you get used to the smell.

Actually, I kind of like the smell, and what's even more important is that the ladies go for it too—well, maybe not a heavy dose but just a little hint behind the ears. And anything that catches the attention of the ladies can't be all bad.

Well, I had me a skunk cornered up in the machine shed and all I had to do was find him—

no big deal. I mean, unless your nose is completely dead, you just switch everything over to instruments and follow your nose.

I found the little feller near the northeast corner of the shed. He was toodling along, sniffing the ground and digging for bugs, and he seemed no more interested in me than if I'd been a fly.

That's the irritating thing about skunks. A cat will run when a dog appears. A chicken will squawk and fly. A skunk will ignore you, which is hard to accept if you happen to be Head of Ranch Security and also impatient.

I'm not famous for my patience, I guess you knew that, and you probably think that I got tired of waiting for Rosebud to leave the machine shed, waded into the middle of him, and got myself sprayed.

Well, the joke's on you. I played that skunk the way a musician would play his instrument, the way a fisherman would play his fish. Using nothing but raw intelligence, superior knowledge, and a whole bagful of cowdog techniques, I applied pressure to Rosebud and oozed him towards the door.

What a piece of work! You should have seen it. When he started to bristle up, I backed off and waited until he settled down. Then I began press-

ing him again until, at last and hoorah, he saw the door and waddled out.

I had never done a better or smoother job of skunking, and I doubt that any dog in history had topped that performance.

When the job was done, Drover suddenly appeared. He of little faith had chosen to wait outside in the fresh air. "Nice work, Hank, you did it! Boy, I couldn't have done that, not in a thousand years."

"Most dogs couldn't have, son. It takes a certain touch and a lot of poise."

"Yeah, 'cause they're poisonous."

"One of these days I'll show you how to do it."

"Oh, that's okay. I'd rather watch."

"Whatever. But the important thing is that we've liberated the machine shed and saved our food supply."

"Sure did. 'Course now he's heading for the house."

"Yes, but that's a small price to pay for . . . WHAT?"

"He's headed for the house. See?"

Drover pointed his nose to the east. My gaze followed a straight line—and I mean like a laser beam—followed a straight line to the yard gate, where I saw Rosebud slip through the fence and enter Sally May's yard.

"Holy smokes, Drover, do you realize what's fixing to happen before our very eyes?"

"Well, let's see."

"Little Alfred left the crawl space uncovered!"

"I'll be derned. What's a scrawl space?"

"It's a hole in the foundation, and it leads to the space under the house. It's common knowledge that skunks love to take up residence under peoples's houses."

"Not me. I'm scared of spiders."

"Drover, at this very moment Loper and Sally May are entertaining all the members of the church choir. Do you realize what might happen if that skunk got under the house and released his poison gas?"

"Well . . . it sure might stink up the party."

"It would ruin the party, Drover. All the guests would have to be evacuated—those that were still alive, that is. Sally May would be heartbroken. Perhaps the family would have to abandon the house and move away."

"Gosh, that's awful."

"Yes, Drover, but the awfulest part is that we have to sit up here and watch the tragedy unfold!"

"Yeah . . . unless we rushed down there and kept him from going under the house."

I stared at him in the moonlight. "What?"

"I said . . . gosh, I don't remember what I said."

"Something about rushing."

"Rushing. Nope, I guess I lost it."

"Hmm. Well, it's a pity that we have to sit here . . . wait a minute! Is there any reason why we're just sitting here? Why couldn't we rush down there and keep the skunk from going under the house?"

"Gee, I never thought of that."

"It might work, Drover, but we'll have to hurry. Are you ready for some combat?"

"Well, I . . . not really."

"What?"

"I said, oh good. Combat. Oh boy."

"That's the spirit. We'll go to Red Alert. I'll meet you at the yard fence."

"Yeah, if this old leg doesn't quit on me."

And with that, we went streaking down the hill towards the fence—to save Sally May's house and Christmas party from complete and total disaster!

I went streaking down to the house, but you know what? On the way something happened. All at once I began to ask myself, "Why am I doing this? Why should I knock myself out for the same woman who recently called me a nincompoop and other hateful things?"

I mean, I was just a "dumb dog," right? The guy who went around eating string all the time, right? And throwing up on ladies' houseshoes because

I didn't have anything better to do with my time, right?

I reached the yard gate and sat down. Who needed it? Not me. Since I was so "dumb," maybe what I needed to do was sit right there and watch the show. It might be fun, watching all the members of the Methodist Church choir evacuate the house when Rosebud went off.

It WOULD be fun, come to think of it: the tenor section jumping through the bedroom window; the sopranos flying out the front door; the altos crawling up the chimney.

Hmmm, yes. It's been said that getting rich is the best revenge. Not true. The best revenge is REVENGE, and never mind the rich part. The best revenge is knowing what's right and then doing what's wrong, out of sheer spite and meanness.

Hey, if Rosebud wanted to blow up the party, who was I to deny him his civil rights? It was a free country and skunks had rights too.

I was sitting there, enjoying delicious wicked thoughts, when Drover came up, huffing and puffing. "Hi, Hank. Did I miss the fight? Boy, this old leg . . ."

"Relax, Drover. We've cancelled the Red Alert. The Security Division has decided to go out on strike."

He stared at me. "What do you mean?"

"I mean, we quit. Let the church choir go out and bark at the skunk. They have such wonderful voices, let's see how well they can do on Skunk Patrol."

"Gosh, I've never heard you talk like that before."

"I know, so let me try to explain it. Listen to this." And before his very eyes, I sang this song.

# 12

# I SAVE THE PARTY AND SALLY MAY LOVES ME AGAIN

### Poor Me

No one appreciates a hero like me.
In spite of the fact that I'm trying to be
Man's very best friend and woman's too,
So what if I happened to barf on her shoe?
My loyalty to her has never ceased,
I've stayed by her side through war and through peace.
I've guarded her kids and chicken coop,
But still she insists I'm a nincompoop.

Well fine, okay, it's a poor-me kind of day.
When you need a friend, just call me and I'll look the other way.
Poor me, poor pay! That's all I have to say.
That's fine, all right, I'm out on strike,
It's a poor-me kind of day.

I bark up the sun most every morn,
I was here at the ranch when her babies were
    born.
I guarded the steaks that she put out to thaw . . .
And maybe I was foolish for eating them raw.
But what of the nights I've stayed up and barked?
And tussled with monsters and things in the
    dark?
Protecting the cattle and chickens and sheep
And got myself shot at for jarring her sleep!

> Well fine, okay, it's a poor-me kind of day.
> When you need a friend, just call me and I'll
>     look the other way.
> Poor me, poor pay! That's all I have to say.
> That's fine, all right, I'm out on strike,
> It's a poor-me kind of day.

So when there is trouble or monsters or stuff,
I plan to be sleeping or warming my duff,
I'll tell them too bad and stay on my seat.
Emergency calls can be handled by Pete.
And then we'll just see what happens from there.
When they're getting their due and getting
    what's fair.
And as the ranch crumbles, I'll cry out with
    glee,
"You've caused this by being so mean to poor me!"

Well fine, okay, it's a poor-me kind of day.
When you need a friend, just call me and I'll look
    the other way.
Poor me, poor pay! That's all I have to say.
That's fine, all right, I'm out on strike,
It's a poor-me kind of day.

The little mutt stared at me in disbelief. "Gosh, I hate to hear you talk like that. Somebody **has** to care . . . about something."

I laughed in his face. "Not me, pal. I'm off duty, and caring isn't in my contract. Let somebody else care."

Just then we heard singing in the house. It was a church song, something about . . . let's see if I can remember the words. Something about . . . here we go:

"Gloria in excelsis Deo,
Et in terra pax hominbus."

It was a lousy song and they were lousy singers, sounded like a barn full of chickens and stray cats. Horrible noise and a stupid song.

They deserved a skunk, all of them.

Drover was listening to the music. "Gosh, that's so pretty! We've never had music like that out here on the ranch."

I curled my lip at him and rolled my eyes. What did HE know about music? Was he some kind of expert on the subject? He didn't even have a decent tail, is what kind of expert he was, only a chopped-off stub.

Okay, maybe the song was a little better than I'd thought, but still . . . pretty good, actually, and there we were, sitting under this deep black sky full of stars, looking out on the whole entire universe that sparkled with ancient light, and the music seemed to be reaching out to the light . . .

Not a bad sound, for a bunch of country people. Pretty good, actually. There they were, doing their little part to make the world a better place, and there I was . . . well, feeling sorry for myself, you might say.

I heaved a big sigh. "Drover, do you know who cares?"

"Nobody, I guess."

"That's where you're wrong. I care. I shouldn't but I do. I can't help it. I guess that just goes with being a cowdog." I pushed myself up. "Come on. We've got a skunk to whip."

"But I thought you said . . ."

"Never mind what I said. There's more to this life than potato soup."

"What does that mean?"

I gazed at him in the starlight. "I'm not sure. It just popped out. Stars were put here to shine. People were put here to sing, and dogs were put here to protect the ranch from skunks. Does that make sense?"

"I guess so."

"Good. Let's move out. We'll have to jump the fence."

"Okay, but this old leg . . ."

I leaped over the fence and made my way around the southwest corner of the house. There, I picked up visual readings of the skunk. He was sniffing around in the iris patch, slowly working his way towards the open crawl space. At his present course, bearing, and speed, he would reach the hole in fifteen seconds.

I went straight to the spot and blocked his path. He waddled forward, raised his head, wiggled his nose, and stared at me with his beady little eyes.

"Scram, Rosebud. The choir's practicing and you need to run along."

As I've already mentioned, skunks don't seem to have any fear of dogs—or much of anything, really—and Rosebud chose to ignore my warning. He had it in his mind to go under the house, and by George, I think he would have walked right between my legs, if I'd let him.

G.L. Holmes

I didn't, of course. I stopped him with a sharp growl. He wiggled his nose and started forward again. This time I stopped him with something more substantial. I clubbed him over the head with a paw.

Suddenly his tail fanned out and he hopped up on his front legs. Then he darted to my left . . . his left . . . he darted to the left and tried to make an end-run on me. At that point, I found it impossible to avoid getting involved.

Over the years, I had tested out several techniques for skunk work, and the one that worked the best was the one I used. I abandoned the soft touch and went to Sterner Measures.

I jumped him, grabbed him behind the neck, and pitched him up into the air.

WHOOSH! SPLAT!

By George, that got his . . . cough, choke, arg . . . attention. All at once he had that tail spread out and he wasn't looking for bugs . . . cough, choke, arg . . . anymore, although it was a little hard for me to see exactly what he was . . . wheeze, arg, snork . . . doing because my eyes were suddenly stinking.

Stinging, that is. But the important thing is that I'd gotten his full undivided attention, and with a skunk, that's important.

Step Two calls for more of the same, only the second time I pitched him towards the yard fence—a not-so-subtle hint that I wanted him to leave. I grabbed him behind the neck and gave him the old heave-ho.

In return, he gave me the old whoosh-splat, and did I say that I kind of like the smell of skunk? Let me back up and rephrase that. A little of that stuff goes a long way, and after a dog has been off Skunk Patrol for a few months, he tends to forget what happened the last time he did it.

In close quarters, in hand-to-hand combat, those guys REALLY STINK. But the nice part about skunking is that once you've taken the first hit, you hardly notice the second, third, and fourth, because that first one knocks out all your sen-

G. L. Holmes

sory equipment, and we're talking about sparks, smoke, shorted wires, blown circuit breakers, and all the lights out on the control panel.

I survived the first hit, lost all my instruments, and kept barking and pitching that little feller away from the house, until he finally got the message.

By that time, the singing inside the house had stopped. Doors flew open and people were outside and I heard them talking about "skunk in the yard" and "pew-weeee!"

Then I heard Sally May's voice above the others. "Loper, your dog has done it again! We can't even have a party without him . . ."

"No, now wait a minute, hon. Look here. Somebody left the crawl space uncovered. Hank kept the skunk from going under the house."

"Oh. You really think so?"

Suddenly I was surrounded by a crowd of admirers. All the members of the church choir had come out into the night to congratulate . . . well, ME, you might say, for heroic actions and service above and below the call of duty.

A few voices stood out above the murmur of the crowd. Let's see if I can remember them:

"What a wonderful dog!"

"Yes, Sally May's so lucky to have him!"

"Gee whiz, I wonder if they'd take a thousand bucks for that dog."

"Oh no, they wouldn't sell Hank, not for any amount of money."

And so forth. I sat there in the middle of the adoring masses, drinking in their praise and trying to appear humble. It was the fulfillment of every cowdog's dream.

But then came the very best part of all. Sally May knelt down beside me—and I mean, right there in front of the whole church choir—knelt down beside me and, you won't believe this, gave me a hug. That's right, hugged my neck and kissed me on the cheek.

"Hank, all these years I've misjudged you. I've been cruel and small-minded and I've ignored the obvious fact that you're probably one of the finest dogs in the whole world. Why, everyone in the choir wants to buy you and take you home. In the last five minutes, we've had three offers of ten thousand dollars cash!

"But we can't let you go, Hank, not for any amount of money. Instead, we want you to move into the house and live with us. I'll fix up the guest bedroom, just for you. We'll move the gas tanks inside, if that's what you want, and spread out your gunnysack on top of the bed.

"We want you to eat your meals with us at the kitchen table—sirloin steak three times a day. And I don't care that you stink. From now on, my house will smell of skunk and dog, and I'll be proud to tell the neighbors that Hank lives with us!"

Well, I couldn't have come up with a better ending for this yarn if I'd written it myself. As a matter of fact, I did, and yes, I might have stretched the truth a bit here and there, but the point is that Sally May was proud of me and I became her hero.

And before we let that pleasant feeling slip away, let's shut this thing down.

Case closed.

And I never did believe Pete's phoney story about the Phantom in the Mirror.

No kidding.

See you around.